THE
SECRET SECRET PASSAGE

Look for these books in the
Clue™ series:

THE
SECRET SECRET PASSAGE

Book created by A. E. Parker

Written by Eric Weiner

Based on characters from the Parker Brothers game

A Creative Media Applications Production

SCHOLASTIC INC.
New York Toronto London Auckland Sydney

*Special thanks to: Thomas Dusenberry,
Julie Ryan, Laura Millhollin, Sandy Upham,
Jean Feiwel, Greg Holch, Dona Smith,
Nancy Smith, John Simko, and Elizabeth Parisi.*

ISBN 0-590-45631-8

12 11 10   5 6 7/9

Printed in the U.S.A.   40

First Scholastic printing, October 1992

For Aaron and Benjamin

Contents

THE
SECRET SECRET PASSAGE

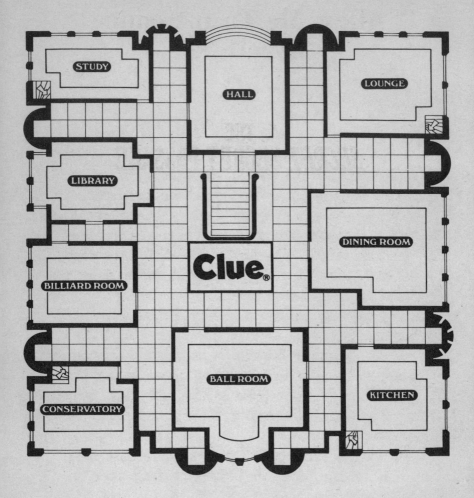

Allow Me To Introduce Myself . . .

I'M YOUR HOST, REGINALD BODDY, AND I'm delighted to have you back at my mansion. *This* time I promise you I won't be murdered.

Perhaps I should explain. As you may recall, the last time you visited me I received a rather nasty knock on the back of the head. But the good news is, I wasn't really dead, just unconscious. I woke up a few hours later.

By the way, my other guests told me what had happened. It was all an accident, they said. You see, the plumber I hired to unplug the Kitchen sink was using a Wrench. Well, it seems that the Wrench slipped out of his hands, flew all the way across the mansion, and hit me on the head in the Library.

Come to think of it, the Wrench must have really hit me hard . . . because I don't even remember hiring a plumber.

Anyway!

You'll be glad to know, I'm having all the same guests back this weekend. After all, they all get along so marvelously! Except, of course, when they're plotting one another's death.

Which reminds me. . . . While you're here, would you mind keeping your eyes peeled? That way, if there should be a little problem — a gruesome, horrifying crime, say — then you could solve it and tell me which guest did it. What do you say?

You have only six suspects to worry about. (I, of course, am never a suspect!) The six suspects are:

Professor Plum: A true genius. Why, he's found the cures for every disease on earth. Unfortunately, he's so absentminded that he's lost every cure two minutes after finding it.

Mrs. Peacock: This kind-hearted woman is so prim and proper she thinks *grime* is a dirty word.

Mr. Green: Some folks call Mr. Green a big bully, but I know better. (I know better than to get myself in trouble by insulting such a big bully!)

Miss Scarlet: A ravishing beauty who never gets jealous. (She's always jealous to begin with.)

Colonel Mustard: Such a brave man. The Colonel is willing to fight a duel against anyone. In fact, he's even dueled *himself*!

Mrs. White: My meek, quiet maid is utterly sweet. I do wish she'd find a different hobby, though. Why would anyone want to collect dangerous weapons?

Don't worry. I'll give you a chart of all the possible suspects, weapons, and rooms at the end of each mystery. As you read, you can check off suspects until you've narrowed your list down to one.

What's that? You say you just heard someone shrieking for help in my Study?! Nonsense!

But, then again, perhaps I *should* go and check. . . .

1.
The *Secret* Secret Passage

In THE STUDY OF MR. BODDY'S MANsion, Professor Plum was peering at the bookcase through his spectacles. Outside, it was pouring. The rain had ruined Plum's croquet match with Colonel Mustard, and Plum was now looking for a good book to pass the afternoon. He spotted one. It was a small black book that he didn't remember ever seeing before.

"The Secret *Secret Passage,"* said Plum, reading the title on the book's spine, "by Roddy Boddy." He reached for it, but the black book was wedged tightly between two others. He had to pull it hard.

"There!" The Professor had the book in his hands. But he only had it for a second because, the instant he removed the book, the entire bookcase spun around, and the book went flying.

The bookcase did a speedy 360° turn. "AYYYYYYY!!" cried Plum as he was whirled around behind the bookcase. He tripped down a short flight of stairs, and fell into the arms of —

A skeleton! Professor Plum screamed again as

the skeleton seemed to dance with him around the passageway.

"Stop it!" cried Plum, pushing it away. The lifeless bones clattered to the stone floor. Professor Plum climbed up the stairs and pushed hard against the back of the bookcase. It didn't budge. He was locked in!

"HELP!" cried Plum. He waited. No response. "HELP!" he cried again.

"Well," he told himself. "I've got to keep calm. Sooner or later, someone will hear me." His glance fell on the skeleton. Obviously, this particular guest had been heard from *later*, not sooner. Plum screamed louder. He pounded on the wall.

Then he heard a strange scurrying sound behind him. He quickly peeked over his shoulder. Two rats had come around the corner of the passageway and were staring up at him with beady red eyes.

"HELP!!" Professor Plum gave a horrible shriek.

Luckily, the horrible shriek was heard by Plum's host, Reginald Boddy. Unluckily, Boddy rushed into the Study, saw that no one was there, and rushed out again.

Now Plum screamed twice as loud, pounded three times as hard, and cried four times more horribly. This time, the noise caught the attention of another guest. A short, pudgy man with gray

5

hair and a green tie peered into the empty Study. "Who's in here?" Mr. Green demanded.

From behind the bookcase, Plum cried, "*I* am!"

"Who is *I*?" Green asked suspiciously.

"How do *I* know who *you* are?" yelled Plum. "I can't see you!"

"I'm sorry," Mr. Green said, turning to leave. "But I don't believe in ghosts."

"WAIT!!"

"Who are you?" Mr. Green asked again.

"Who am I?" Professor Plum thought for a moment. Then, he had it. "Professor Plum!"

"Professor Plum?! Where are you?"

"Behind the bookcase. Listen, do you see a book lying somewhere on the floor?"

Mr. Green glanced down at the dark red carpet and spotted the small black book.

"Yes!" said Green.

"Put it back on the shelf."

Green picked up the book and was about to do as the professor asked. Suddenly, he stopped. His narrow eyes narrowed even more. "Listen, Plum, this better not be some kind of a trick," he sneered. "I don't have time for games."

"It's not a game. Just put the book back."

Mr. Green wedged the small book back into the only open space. Then he screamed.

Because the bookcase had spun again. This

time, Green was thrown on top of the skeleton. And Plum found himself back in the Study.

"That's odd!" exclaimed Plum, looking around the empty room. "I wonder where he went!"

Just then, the grandfather clock swung open as Miss Scarlet entered through the secret passageway from the Kitchen. When she saw Plum, her face turned red. Then she giggled flirtatiously. "You won't tell Mr. Boddy, will you?" she asked, tossing back her shiny dark hair.

"Tell him what?" asked Plum.

"Well, Reginald doesn't like his guests to use the secret passageways. He thinks they're dangerous." She gave Plum's purple bow tie a spin. "It'll be our little-wittle secret, what do you say, my poochie-woochie?"

"Goo-goo, ga-ga?" asked Plum.

There was a muffled scream.

"What was that?" Miss Scarlet asked with alarm.

Plum slapped his forehead. "That reminds me of what I wanted to tell you. I've just discovered a *secret* secret passage. One that nobody else knows about."

There was another scream. "Someone is screaming behind this bookcase," Miss Scarlet said.

"That's right!" said Plum triumphantly.

7

"You've found the *secret* secret passage." He pointed to the tiny black book. "Pull that book out and you'll get a wonderful surprise."

Miss Scarlet did as she was told. Then she screamed and went flying. So did the book. The bookcase had spun her out of the room and brought back Mr. Green. Strange, thought Plum, Mr. Green looks furious.

"No games, you said!" yelled Mr. Green. Then he started to chase Plum around the room.

"Sorry," cried Plum as he ran. "I didn't mean any harm."

"Well," yelled Green, looking around for a weapon, "I *do!*"

He bent down to pick up the brass poker from the fireplace. At least, he tried to pick it up. Instead, the poker bent like a lever when he pulled it. A bell rang. A cloud of smoke coughed out from the fireplace, and the whole thing quickly spun 360°. Mr. Green, who was still holding the poker, was whooshed right out of the room.

Unaware of what had happened, Professor Plum was still running in circles, yelling, "Help! Save me! Stop!"

Colonel Mustard entered and studied Plum through his monocle. "What seems to be the problem, old boy?"

"Oh, please don't hurt me!" answered Plum, running faster.

"Stop!" shouted Mustard, chasing after the professor.

"I will, I will!" promised Plum. "I'll never do it again!"

Then he screamed in terror, because Mustard had caught him. He turned. And almost fainted. "Mr. Green!" cried the professor. "You look so much like Colonel Mustard!"

"I *am* Mustard!"

"You are?" Plum thought this over. "Well then, why are *you* chasing me?"

"To find out why you were running in circles," said Mustard breathlessly. Plum looked blank. "Why were you running in circles?" repeated the Colonel.

Plum shook his head. "I have no idea."

There was now a strange pounding from behind both the bookcase and the fireplace. Mustard whirled around, surprised. He started toward the bookcase and stepped on something. He picked up the small black book.

"Oh yes!" yelled Plum. "Now I remember. That book belongs on the shelf!"

Mustard started to put the book back, but the bookcase spun around once more and the book flew out of his hand. Mustard disappeared. Miss Scarlet reappeared. "Is this how you treat a beautiful woman?" she yelled. And she started chasing Plum around the room.

9

She stopped to pick up a weapon, and reached for the same brass poker from the fireplace. The bell rang and the cloud of smoke coughed out from the fireplace. And now it was Mr. Green who was, once again, chasing Plum. (Miss Scarlet, of course, had vanished behind the fireplace.)

Green dove for his prey. But just at that moment, the professor forgot why he was running around in circles. He came to a dead halt.

That caused Green to miss him completely. He zoomed right by, did a flying somersault, and landed in the plush red side chair. He landed so hard that his head flew back and hit a tiny gold button. A buzzer sounded, and the whole chair flipped up into the wall. When the chair came back down, Mr. Green was gone. Once again, Professor Plum found himself in an empty Study.

For a moment, he couldn't remember what he was doing. Then, suddenly, he remembered everything.

It was raining outside. He had come into the Study to find a good book to read! He picked up *The* Secret *Secret Passage*, sat down in the red side chair and, with a contented sigh, began to read.

"Allow me to introduce myself," began the book. "My name is Roderick Boddy, but you can call me Roddy."

"Hello, Roddy," said Plum. He checked the

book's date. It must have been written by his host's great-grandfather.

"Now that my mansion is complete," Plum read on, "I thought I had better write down some of its secrets, in case anything should happen to me. I'm so rich, you see, that I live in fear of attack at all times. Everyone wants to steal my treasure and they'll stop at nothing. That's why I've rigged the place with all kinds of traps and escape routes for my own protection."

Plum read on eagerly. He read about the *secret* secret passageway behind the bookcase. He read about the *secret* secret passageway behind the fireplace. He read about the *secret* secret passageway behind the red chair. (It was a little hard to read with all the screaming and pounding that was going on, but he forced himself to concentrate.) He also read about a *secret* secret circular passageway that connected all the *secret* secret passageways with the secret passage behind the grandfather clock.

"Ignoring me by reading?!" exclaimed a shrill voice. "How rude!"

Mrs. Peacock had entered the room.

Plum threw the book up in surprise. It opened and landed on his bald head, and sat like a hat. "Sorry," said Plum. "I didn't know you were here. And this book is so fascinating. Here. Have a look."

11

He removed the book from his head and showed her the diagrams of the *secret* secret passageways. As they talked, the guest who had been trapped behind the bookcase found the *secret* secret circular passage and followed it to the grandfather clock. Meanwhile, the guest who was behind the fireplace followed the same circular passage and ended up behind the red chair. The guest who was behind the red chair also followed the passage and wound up behind the bookcase.

The missing guests all pounded hard at the same time. "What's that pounding?" asked a horrified Mrs. Peacock.

Plum thought hard, and then said, "I don't know." He flipped through the book. "I'll check the index under 'pounding' for an explanation."

Meanwhile, the guest behind the grandfather clock continued along the passageway to the fireplace. The guest behind the red chair stayed put. And the guest behind the bookcase traveled on to the grandfather clock.

"Nothing about pounding," said Plum.

"How about a cup of hot cocoa?" asked Mrs. White, the maid, who had just entered carrying a silver tray.

"Oh, how wonderful," said Mrs. Peacock. "Cocoa is just the thing on a cold rainy day like today."

"Too bad," said Mrs. White sweetly. "I only

brought tea." Then she turned her back and laughed with bitter delight. She turned back toward her guests again, and her face began to quiver with fear.

The grandfather clock was swinging open, and someone was aiming a Revolver at Plum!

WHO IS ABOUT TO SHOOT PLUM?

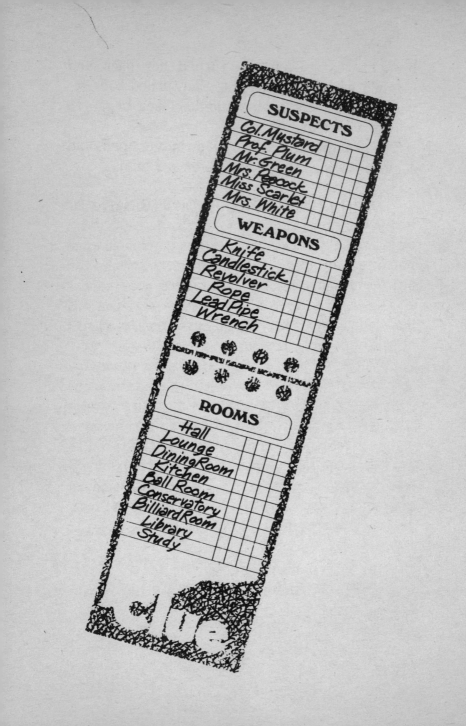

SOLUTION

MR. GREEN in the STUDY with the REVOLVER

When Mrs. Peacock entered, Mustard was be-hind the bookcase, Miss Scarlet was behind the fireplace, and Green was behind the chair. First, Mustard moved to the grandfather clock, Scarlet to the chair, and Green to the bookcase.

Then, the guest behind the bookcase (Mr. Green) moved to the grandfather clock. So when the grandfather clock swung open, it was Mr. Green aiming the Revolver.

By the way, the shot missed Plum, but hit the tiny gold button behind the red chair, which rang the buzzer and brought back Miss Scarlet. The second shot also missed, but it zinged into the brass poker, bent the lever, rang the bell, coughed out a cloud of smoke, and delivered Mustard. The three guests forgave Plum. Then they chased him out of the room.

2.
The Challenge

"**I** CHALLENGE YOU TO A DUEL!" shouted Colonel Mustard in the Conservatory.

"But there's no one in here," said Mrs. White, the maid, sticking her head into the room and staring at Mustard in wonder. "You're talking to yourself!"

"Talking to myself!" Mustard turned yellow. "Are you calling me *silly*?" He pointed the finger of one yellow-gloved hand in the air. "I challenge *you* to a duel!"

Mrs. White laughed and waved her feather duster in the air like a sword. "You're on!"

But Mustard stormed past her. "Choose a 'second,'" he said.

"A second what?" asked Mrs. White.

"A 'second' is a person who will help you get ready before you fight," said Colonel Mustard. "Follow me! We'll battle it out in the Ball Room!"

He charged toward the Ball Room. But Mrs. White continued to giggle. Mustard turned back with fury, which meant that he wasn't looking where he was going. He bumped smack into Professor Plum.

"Getting in my way, eh?" cried Mustard. He pulled off one of his yellow gloves and slapped Plum on the nose with it. "This means a duel!"

"A duel? . . . but I . . . ah . . . "

"Don't mind him," Mrs. White called to the professor. "The Colonel seems to have woken up on the wrong side of the bed this morning."

"Are you implying that I don't know which side of the bed to wake up on?" the Colonel huffed. "I challenge you to a duel!"

"You already challenged me," said Mrs. White dryly. She followed Plum and Mustard into the Ball Room, dusting the mansion's dark wooden panelling as she went. Inside, Mrs. Peacock was sitting on the red love seat, reading a book.

"Anyway, Colonel," continued Mrs. White, "we all know you're just in a bad mood because you finished last in Mr. Boddy's tiddlywinks tournament."

"Calling me a sore loser, eh?" said Mustard. "I challenge you to a duel."

"Oh, not again, Colonel," said plump Mrs. Peacock, looking up from her book, *How to Behave Properly While Asleep.*

"Yes, really, Colonel," said Plum. "Dueling is a serious business. And you're always willing to

17

fight a duel at the drop of a hat."

Mrs. Peacock took off her blue hat with its tall peacock feather. "Yes," she said, "it's a lucky thing I never drop *my* hat."

Which was exactly when she lost her grip on the hat. She juggled it for a moment, and then it flew into the air and landed . . .

Right on Colonel Mustard's head.

At the sight of Mustard wearing the tall peacock-feathered cap, Mrs. White, Professor Plum, and Mrs. Peacock all burst out laughing.

"Laughing at me?!" cried Mustard. "I challenge you all to a duel!"

"Oh, dear," said Mr. Boddy as he entered the Ball Room. "No duels, please, Colonel. I want all my guests to get along in peace."

"Are you saying I fight too many duels? I challenge you to a duel!"

"I wasn't saying you fight too many duels," Mr. Boddy said gently. "It's just that I don't want you to fight *any*."

Colonel Mustard stared at Boddy for a moment. "Trying to be nice, eh?" he finally shouted. "I challenge you to a duel for being nice!" Everyone stared at him in shock. "Hmm," Colonel Mustard continued, "that doesn't seem like a very good reason for a duel, does it?"

A tiny smile began to curl up under his mustache. The other guests smiled back at him. His own smile broadened. He began to laugh. Then to chortle. And at last to guffaw. "I can't believe I was challenging you to a duel for being nice," Mustard said, shaking his head as he roared with laughter. He threw an arm around his shorter host's sloping shoulder. "Oh, Mr. Boddy, you must forgive me."

Mr. Boddy laughed, too. "No harm done. No harm done at all."

"I guess I *was* a little steamed up about losing that tiddlywinks tournament," added Mustard.

"Losing!" said Mr. Green as he strolled into the Ball Room. "You came in dead last." Tucked under his right arm was a tall, silver trophy. On top of it was a little silver figure tossing tiddlywinks. FIRST PLACE, read the trophy's inscription.

"Now, now," said Mr. Boddy, looking worried. "Let's not rub salt in the wound."

"Yes," said Professor Plum with a quick wink. "Someone may already be in a very bad mood."

"Someone who has a *duel* nature," added Mrs. Peacock.

"Someone you're afraid of," said Mrs. White.

"Nonsense," said Mr. Green. "I fear no one." He set his trophy on top of the grand piano and stared at it lovingly. "Gee, Mustard, I really beat the pants off you today, didn't I? I'm glad to see you've put on a new pair."

Colonel Mustard's mustache began to twitch.

19

"Colonel Mustard," said Mr. Boddy. "There's something I've been meaning to talk to you about." He linked his arm through the Colonel's. "It's a small matter of a huge amount of money I'd like to give you. Perhaps we could talk it over in the Library?"

"And I've got a cake I baked for you in the Kitchen," said Mrs. White, taking the Colonel's other arm.

"And I've got a brainteaser for you," added Plum, pulling the Colonel's tie.

"And I was hoping you'd read to me from my manners book," said Mrs. Peacock, pulling on the Colonel's ear.

"Yes, yes," said the Colonel, following them all toward the door. "I'd better leave. If I stay here I'm liable to lose my temper."

"*Lose* your temper?" said Mr. Green. "I didn't know you had ever found it." He chuckled. "You were quite a sight, jumping up and down on those tiddlywinks."

Suddenly, the Colonel broke free from the other guests. "That does it! You have insulted me one too many times!" The Colonel's eyes blazed. "MR. GREEN! I CHALLENGE YOU TO A DUEL!"

Mr. Green smiled ever so slightly. "You dare to challenge *me*?"

"Now, now, gentlemen," Mr. Boddy said, pushing the two guests apart. "I'm sure we can settle this in a gentlemanly way."

"I'm sure we can," agreed Mustard, "because gentlemen settle their arguments . . . by *dueling*. Choose your second, Mr. Green."

"Miss Scarlet," Mr. Green said as Miss Scarlet waltzed into the room, "will you be my second?"

"Your second?" Miss Scarlet sniffed. "I am every man's *first* love, no one's second. But, yes, I will."

"Plum," said Colonel Mustard. "Will you do me the honor of being my second?"

"Colonel, please stop this," Mr. Boddy interrupted.

But it was no use. The duel was on.

"I can't watch," Mr. Boddy cried, rushing from the room.

"Neither can I," said Mrs. Peacock, hurrying after him. "Dueling is so rude!"

"You'd better leave us as well, Mrs. White," said Colonel Mustard, "for your own safety." He held the door open for the maid, then locked it behind her.

"All right," he said to Mr. Green. "Let's choose our weapons."

Six weapons were laid out on top of the grand piano: the Knife, the Revolver, the Wrench, the Candlestick, the Lead Pipe, and the Rope. They took turns choosing.

"According to the international rules of gentlemanly dueling," said Mustard, "we will each choose three weapons. We will then use each weapon once and only once. Agreed?"

"Agreed," said Green.

"Seconds," Mustard continued, "*you* are here to make sure everyone follows the rules."

Miss Scarlet and Professor Plum both nodded nervously.

"All right, then," Mustard said. "Let's begin."

"You know," Mr. Green said, beginning to tremble, "I can't really remember what we were dueling about. Maybe we can just shake —"

"You're shaking already," said Mustard. "Please remember you're a gentleman! True gentlemen don't shake."

"But at least I'm a living gentleman," said Mr. Green, "and I'd like to remain —"

"Mr. Green!" cried Mustard. "The time for speeches has ended! Prepare to die."

Mr. Green and Colonel Mustard stood back-to-back. "We'll count off twenty paces," said Mustard. He and Green each took a giant step. "One!" Mustard called.

Mrs. White, who was peeping through the door's keyhole from the hallway, now turned to Mr. Boddy and Mrs. Peacock and said, "They're counting off twenty paces."

"I can't watch," Mr. Boddy said, and he covered his eyes.

"Neither can I," said Mrs. Peacock, covering her eyes as well.

Mrs. White stared at them. "What's the matter with you two? You can't see anything to begin with. We're outside the room, remember?"

"But I can see them in my mind's eye," said Mr. Boddy, still covering his eyes. "And that's bad enough."

"Eight!" counted Mustard, taking another giant step. "Nine! Ouch!"

"Ouch!" yelled Green, as well.

"What happened?" gasped Mrs. Peacock and Mr. Boddy in unison.

Mrs. White put her eye back to the keyhole. "They took too many paces," she explained. "They both smacked into the wall."

Now Mustard and Green slowly turned to face each other. Mr. Green was trembling all over. So was Miss Scarlet, who stood by his side. So was Plum, who stood next to the Colonel. Mr. Green slowly raised the Knife in the air. He threw it hard.

He missed Mustard, but he hit Plum.

"Plum's been hit!" cried Mrs. White at the keyhole.

"Plum?" asked Mr. Boddy and Mrs. Peacock.

Inside the Ball Room, Mr. Green was shaking even more violently now. Because Colonel Mustard was slowly lowering the Revolver until it pointed right at Green. Then he squeezed the trigger. BANG!

"He missed!" cried Mrs. White.

"Thank goodness," said Boddy and Peacock.

"He didn't miss me," yelled Miss Scarlet. She began to stagger around the room. She bumped into Professor Plum, who was also staggering around the room. Now the two seconds staggered around the room together.

"It's Mr. Green's turn again," announced Mrs. White from outside the door. "He's swinging . . . he's swinging the —" There was the sound of someone banging a loud chord on the piano. Mrs. White pressed her eye harder against the keyhole. "It was either the Wrench, the golden Candlestick, or the Lead Pipe," she told Mr. Boddy. "It happened so fast I couldn't be sure."

"Never mind which weapon," cried Boddy. "What happened?"

Mrs. White stared back into the room. "He missed. But he played a smash hit on the grand piano."

"Now what's happening?" Mrs. Peacock cried.

"I can't really see," said Mrs. White. "Miss

Scarlet just staggered in front the keyhole. Now Plum staggered by. Now Miss Scarlet again. Aha! There's Mustard. It's his turn now. He's got the Rope. He's making it into a lasso. And —"

From inside the Ball Room came a tremendous crash. Mr. Boddy held his breath. He also held Mrs. Peacock's. "What happened?" he finally gasped.

"He missed Green," explained the maid. "But he caught the chandelier."

"My chandelier?" Mr. Boddy exclaimed. "It's a priceless antique."

"Don't worry," said Mrs. White. "It's not broken. Now Mr. Green's swinging either the Wrench or the Revolver."

There was a loud crash. "*Now* the chandelier is broken," Mrs. White said.

"Well, Mr. Green," said Mustard. "It seems we're down to the final weapon."

"I apologize if I offended you," Mr. Green said. "Very very very much."

"That's not much," said Mustard, raising his last weapon.

Outside the door, Mrs. White glimpsed a flash. She couldn't see what was flashing, except to say that it was not golden.

This time, Mr. Green ducked. Unfortunately, Mustard's aim was low. So when Green ducked, he got hit. Green fell to the floor with a groan. Miss Scarlet staggered over and fell on top of him. Then Plum landed on top of them both.

"I win," said Colonel Mustard simply.

WHICH WEAPON DID COLONEL MUSTARD USE LAST?

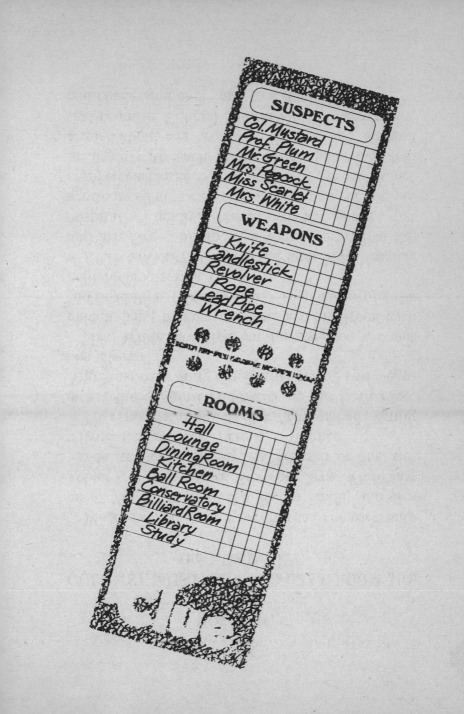

SOLUTION

COLONEL MUSTARD in the BALL ROOM with the LEAD PIPE

We know that each weapon was to be used only once. We know that the Rope, Knife, and Revolver have been used. So, when Mrs. White saw Green swinging either the Wrench or the Revolver, it must have been the Wrench.

That means that, earlier, Green had swung either the golden Candlestick or the Lead Pipe. And Mustard swung one of these same two weapons later.

Mrs. White saw that the last weapon was not golden. That means that Mustard hit Green with the Lead Pipe. (Earlier, Mr. Green had swung the golden Candlestick.)

After the duel, Professor Plum, Miss Scarlet, and Mr. Green all spent a week together in the hospital. Luckily, their wounds were just scratches. They mended quickly and, of course, enjoyed each other's company. They promised not to argue with each other ever again, and then argued about who would be the first one to break that promise. Colonel Mustard lost the argument, and challenged everyone to a duel.

3.
The Joke Contest

MR. BODDY TINKLED THE SILVER bell at the head of the long table and gazed at his dinner guests with obvious delight.

"I've just remembered the joke I wanted to tell all of you." He burst out laughing.

"Mr. Boddy," began Mrs. Peacock, "I don't want to be rude. But it is customary to *tell* the joke. Not just to laugh at it yourself."

"I know, I know," Mr. Boddy said, wiping away tears of merriment. "It's just —" He started laughing again. "It's just that it's . . . so funny."

He pulled himself together. "All right. Here it is. What's black and white and red all over?"

"A newspaper," the guests all said.

"No, a sunburned zebra!" yelled Mr. Boddy, slapping the table and laughing like crazy. The guests chuckled politely.

"That reminds me of a joke," Mr. Green told the group. "What did the silly man name his zebra?"

"What?" everyone asked.

"Spot."

There were more chuckles this time than for Boddy's joke, but only a few more.

"I don't get it," said Mr. Boddy. "Wouldn't Stripe be a more appropriate name?"

"Here's one," said Miss Scarlet. "What's black and white and has sixteen wheels? . . . A zebra on roller skates."

Miss Scarlet's joke received the most laughter so far. Her cheeks flushed scarlet with pleasure.

Mrs. White had just come in carrying a tray of pastries.

"Knock, knock," she said.

"Who's there?" asked the guests.

"Wiener," said Mrs. White.

"Wiener who?" asked the guests.

"Wiener you going to open the door so I can bring in these pastries?"

The guests whooped.

"Does your undershirt have holes in it?" Colonel Mustard asked Professor Plum.

"I forget," said Plum.

Mustard turned away in disgust. "How about *your* undershirt?" he asked Mr. Green. "Does it have holes in it?"

"No," said Mr. Green, "of course not."

"Then how did you put it on this morning?"

No one laughed.

"*You* ruined the timing," Mustard told Plum.

"Oh, that reminds me of another joke," said

Miss Scarlet. She turned to Mrs. Peacock. "Ask me what my job is and then ask me what the hardest thing about it is."

"What's your job?" Mrs. Peacock asked with a little giggle.

"I'm a stand-up comic."

"And what's the hardest —"

"Timing," said Miss Scarlet at the wrong time. Everyone hooted.

"Isn't it great that we're all having such a wonderful time?" said Mr. Boddy.

He spoke too soon.

"Well," said Miss Scarlet. "It's certainly clear who the wittiest one is around *here*."

Mr. Green smiled proudly. So did Mrs. White.

"Obviously," Miss Scarlet said, "it's me."

Mr. Green fumed. So did Mrs. White.

"Well, it's not like I'm boasting," Miss Scarlet said, daintily daubing her bright red lipstick with a napkin. "Everyone laughed at my jokes the most."

"That's the funniest thing you've said so far," snarled Green. "Everyone laughed hardest at *my* joke."

"Yes," said Mrs. White. "I've got a funny bone to pick with you myself. I thought *I* was the funniest."

"You? Funny?" said Miss Scarlet with a bitter laugh. "You're about as funny as a funeral."

"Now, now," Mr. Boddy said. "You're *all* funny. Ah, Mrs. White? The coffee and tea?"

"No, thank you," Miss Scarlet said, standing. "I won't stay in this room a second longer until everyone admits that I was the funniest."

"Never!" shouted Green.

"Not even then!" added Mrs. White.

"Let's put it to a vote," Miss Scarlet snapped.

"A vote?" Mr. Boddy said nervously. "Oh, I don't think that's such a good idea. You see —"

"A secret vote," added Miss Scarlet. "So no one's feelings will be hurt and everyone can tell the truth."

"Good idea." Mrs. White began placing tiny white napkins next to each of the guests. "We can use these for ballots. Vote for Mr. Green, Miss Scarlet, or me."

"Oh no," Mr. Boddy said, but all the guests were already taking out pens and pencils. They glanced at each other warily to make sure no one was peeking.

"After you've voted, fold the napkin in half and pass it to Mr. Boddy," Miss Scarlet instructed, her dark eyes flashing with excitement.

The napkin ballots were passed to Boddy. "Where's *your* napkin?" Mr. Green asked his host.

"Oh, I abstain, I abstain," Mr. Boddy said. "You were all so funny that —"

"Never mind that," Mr. Green interrupted. "Just count the votes."

"Oh, dear. Let's see here."

He began to count. The room grew silent. Finally, Mr. Boddy looked up. "The winner," he said, "is . . ."

"Is . . ." prompted the guests.

"Mrs. White."

Mrs. White clapped her hands with delight. "I'm the funniest! I'm the funniest!" She jumped up and down with excitement.

"Well, I don't know about *that*," said Mr. Green, "but I guess it's okay, as long as that braggart Miss Scarlet didn't win."

Miss Scarlet was pacing up and down the Dining Room like a caged cat. "I was robbed! I was robbed!"

"What did they take?" Professor Plum asked.

"Robbed of the election, you fool," she hissed. "I demand a recount."

Boddy bent his head over the napkins and counted again. "Two for Mr. Green . . ." he muttered. He looked up fearfully. "No, Mrs. White is still the winner."

"Whoever voted against me," simmered Miss Scarlet, "let me tell you right now. I will get revenge."

"Luckily for all of us," said Colonel Mustard,

"you will never know who voted for whom. That's exactly why we had a secret ballot."

Miss Scarlet yanked her long dark hair and yelled in frustration.

But suddenly, a smile crossed her face. "Wait a minute. I know that each contestant voted for herself . . . or himself. That means . . ." She eyed the frightened guests, one by one. "That means I know exactly who voted against me."

WHO VOTED AGAINST MISS SCARLET?

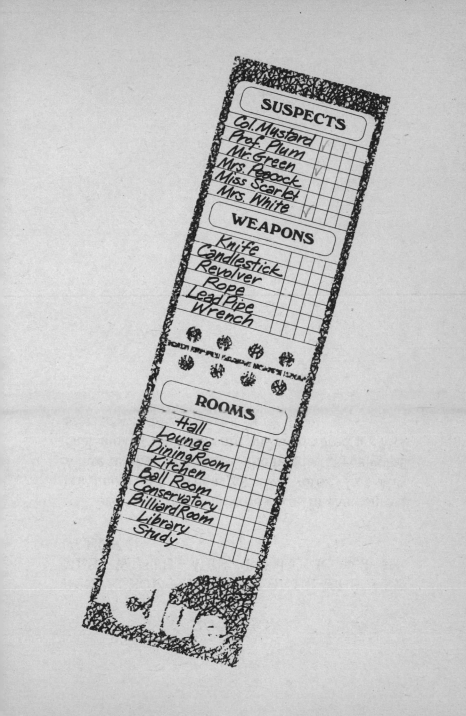

SOLUTION

PROFESSOR PLUM, COLONEL MUSTARD, MRS. WHITE, MRS. PEACOCK, and MR. GREEN

There were only six votes cast in the contest. We know Mr. Green got two votes. For Mrs. White to beat that score, she needed three votes. That means that the only one who voted for Miss Scarlet was Miss Scarlet herself.

4.
Mrs. White's Horrible Plan

Grimacing with anger, Mrs. White pushed open the door to the Lounge and wheeled in a tray of milk and cookies. When she came through the door, she was smiling sweetly. "Snacktime," she told the five guests who were gathered inside. The guests all looked up, surprised. Each held a pen.

"Oh, thank you!" Mr. Boddy told his maid. He put his arm around her shoulder. "Isn't she the most thoughtful maid in the world?"

"Yes!" agreed the guests.

Mrs. White lowered her eyes. "Oh," she said, "you're too kind." She turned away, as if overcome with emotion. But if anyone had glanced in the mirror at that moment, they would have seen the reflection of Mrs. White's face and seen that she was scowling horribly.

"As a matter of fact," Mr. Boddy said, "we were just talking about you."

Mrs. White turned back smiling. "Yes?"

"Well, yes," Mr. Boddy began, beaming. "You see, we've all just made a change in our wills."

For the first time, Mrs. White noticed the pa-

37

pers each of the guests was holding.

"We've each left you something," Mrs. Peacock added.

Mrs. White gasped. The guests grinned. "I'm overwhelmed," she said.

"We've each left you some household chores to do," said Miss Scarlet. "Ha-ha, just joking."

"No, seriously," said Colonel Mustard. "I don't want to go into exact figures, but the sums are — well, considerable."

"Yes, if anything should happen to us —" Professor Plum began.

"Not that it will, of course —" Mrs. Peacock threw in.

"But if anything should, then . . . then . . ." The Professor began to stammer. "Then I forget what would happen!"

"Then you'll be well taken care of," Colonel Mustard finished. "I can assure you."

"You'll have maids working for *you*," agreed Mr. Green.

"Dozens of them," said Miss Scarlet with a grin.

"Oh, my goodness — thank you all so much!" gushed the maid. "How thoughtful!"

Mrs. White was smiling broadly. And when she turned her back, she was still smiling.

For in that instant, she had formed a plan. A horrible plan.

And later that night . . .

And later that night, alone in her maid's room,
Mrs. White went over her sinister scheme.

First, she gathered together all six weapons.
Having made up the beds for years, Mrs. White
knew the guests' sleeping arrangements by heart.
Because the roof had recently been leaking, the
guests were sleeping in the main rooms of the
mansion. She jotted down each guest's temporary
room on a piece of paper:

Mr. Boddy	Billiard Room
Mr. Green	Lounge
Mrs. Peacock	Study
Miss Scarlet	Ball Room
Colonel Mustard	Conservatory
Professor Plum	Library

Next she drew a chart. She would kill each
sleeping guest with the following weapons:

Mr. Boddy	The Wrench
Mr. Green	The Rope
Mrs. Peacock	The Knife
Miss Scarlet	The Revolver
Colonel Mustard	The Lead Pipe
Professor Plum	The Candlestick

Mrs. White dotted the final *i* in Candlestick. Her look of fury now changed back to a smile. She was ready to go into action. The money would soon be hers.

Meanwhile, the guests were all getting ready for bed. Or trying to. Mr. Green didn't like his room. So he switched with Professor Plum.

And Professor Plum then switched with Miss Scarlet, who had already switched with Mrs. Peacock.

At the same time, in the small cramped maid's room, Mrs. White was scowling as she sharpened the Knife, which she planned to use on her first victim.

She could hear the snores of the guests.

Everyone in the mansion was asleep now. . . .

Except Mrs. White.

There was only one last thing to do. She picked up the piece of paper on which she had written her chart. She memorized it carefully. Then she lit a match to it.

She watched the fire curl the edges of the paper. At the same time, a terrible smile curled the edges of her mouth. There would be no evidence to link her to the crimes that were about to occur.

Moving quietly on slippered feet, the murderess now headed toward her first victim . . .

WHOM DID MRS. WHITE STAB?

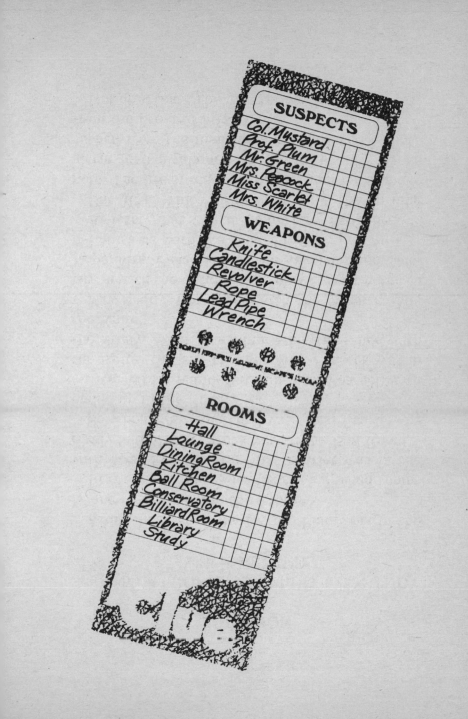

SOLUTION

She stabbed PROFESSOR PLUM in the STUDY with the KNIFE.

After the first room switch, Plum was in the Lounge and Green in the Library.

In the meantime, Miss Scarlet switched rooms with Mrs. Peacock. So Miss Scarlet was in the Study and Mrs. Peacock was in the Ball Room. So when Plum switched with Miss Scarlet, he ended up in the Study.

Mrs. White planned to kill Mrs. Peacock with the Knife. But she thought Mrs. Peacock was in the Study. So it was Plum who was killed with the Knife.

Mr. Boddy was killed with the Wrench, Mr. Green with the Candlestick, Miss Scarlet with the Rope, Mrs. Peacock with the Revolver, and Colonel Mustard with the Lead Pipe.

At least, that's what *would* have happened. But Mrs. White forgot one thing: the burning note. The fire spread, set off the mansion's smoke alarm, and awakened all the guests. Everyone rushed from the mansion and was saved — both from the fire *and* Mrs. White.

Not only that. The guests saw that Mrs. White

had all the weapons, and they became suspicious. After the fire was put out, everyone wrote her out of their wills. Mrs. White would have to continue to serve as Mr. Boddy's bitter maid.

5.
Boddy Language

Dear Mrs. Peacock,

Please do me the honor of attending a special screening of a movie at my mansion on Monday, October 11, at 8:00 P.M.

The film is called *Boddy Language*. It's a murder mystery about a man who can't talk. And best of all, I helped produce it. I hope to see you there!

Your fond host,
Reginald Boddy

"Fond host indeed," raved Mrs. Peacock as she reread the note. Then she banged the brass door knocker with all her might.

She was standing on the front porch of Mr. Boddy's mansion. Mrs. White, the maid, opened the door. "Hello, ma'am," Mrs. White said with a smile and a curtsy. "You're the first to arrive. How nice to see you." But behind her back, Mrs. White crossed her fingers and mouthed, "Not!"

Mrs. Peacock stormed past her. "Where is that scoundrel?"

"What scoundrel is that, ma'am?"

"You know very well who I mean. Your rude employer, Mr. —"

Mr. Boddy had just come into the hall. He was wearing a tuxedo and a broad grin. "Mrs. Peacock! I'm so happy you could come!"

"Mr. Boddy!" Mrs. Peacock said, spitting out each word.

Mr. Boddy wiped his face with his hanky. "Is there a problem?"

Mrs. Peacock held up her invitation. "You don't really intend to show this smut tonight, do you?"

"Well, yes," said Mr. Boddy. Lines of worry creased his face, and then his clothes as well.

"But . . . but . . . " sputtered Mrs. Peacock.

"But what?"

"But I hear it's got a scene where a white horse walks through a mud puddle. Filth!"

"Oh, so that's the problem." Mr. Boddy's face relaxed. "Mrs. Peacock, you really are very prim and proper, aren't you? I can assure you, there's nothing objectionable in this film at all. Do you think I would have invested my own money in the project if there were?"

Mrs. Peacock clasped her hands together. She begged Mr. Boddy to cancel the movie, but he politely refused.

"Then I will have to stop the screening myself," Mrs. Peacock said simply.

"But you can't do that," Mr. Boddy said, shocked.

"Believe me, I can," said Mrs. Peacock. "And I will."

Twenty minutes later . . .

Twenty minutes later, the other guests had arrived and were gathered in the Library for the screening.

"Before we begin," began Mr. Boddy, "I'd like to say a few words, if I can."

"If you *may*," corrected Mrs. Peacock bitterly.

"If I may."

"There now," joked Mustard. "You've said your few words. Now on with the show."

"Ha-ha," said Mr. Boddy, forcing a polite laugh. "But you see, the thing is, I'm just so excited for you all to see this movie. It's the first film I helped finance. And, well, you are my dearest friends. I treasure your opinions above all others. And, well, I do hope you'll like it."

"It's filth," said Mrs. Peacock flatly.

"But you haven't seen it yet," Mr. Boddy gently reminded her.

"I don't need to see it. I won't see it . . . and neither will any of you."

"Yes, well, we'll just see about that," said Mr. Boddy. "Mrs. White? Lights, please."

Mrs. White flicked the light switch. Mr. Boddy made his way through the dark room to the projector and got the film started. The credits rolled across the screen — the actors, the writers, the director, the crew. And then, the final credit:

Gave Lots of Money . . . Reginald Boddy

The guests cheered. All except Mrs. Peacock, of course.

Then the movie began.

In the movie, the man who could not talk was played by an actor dressed as a mime. He carried a Wrench and stalked his first victim.

At the same time, Mrs. Peacock removed the Wrench she had hidden in her pocket and stalked the film projector.

In the movie, the police caught the silent killer and tied him up with Rope.

In the audience, Mrs. White spotted Mrs. Peacock as she tiptoed toward the projector. She nudged Mr. Boddy, and the two of them were able to catch Mrs. Peacock and tie *her* up with the Rope.

In the movie, the killer cleverly made it seem as if he were tied up more tightly than he really

47

was. Then he escaped easily. Mrs. Peacock did the same thing.

In the movie, a white hole appeared in the picture. It grew bigger.

That was because Mrs. Peacock was now using one of the six weapons to burn a hole in the film!

"Stop that!" cried Mr. Green, who was really enjoying the movie. He grabbed Mrs. Peacock and managed to pry the weapon away from her. The movie continued.

In the movie, the killer tried to throw a Knife at another victim. At the same time, in Mr. Boddy's dark Library, Mrs. Peacock threw the Knife at the film projector.

In the movie, the mime missed. So did Mrs. Peacock. Instead, she sliced off one half of Plum's bow tie.

In the movie, the police wrestled the Knife away from the mime. And in the audience, the guests all wrestled the Knife away from Mrs. Peacock. They tried to hold her, but she wriggled free. They began to chase her around the dark room.

"I've got her!" exclaimed Mustard.

The first reel of the film had ended. The screen was white. And as the rest of the guests watched, they now saw a strange sight on the blank screen. Mustard's silhouette was wrestling with the silhouette of the plump Mrs. Peacock. Mustard managed to pry loose the silhouette of a short weapon from Mrs. Peacock's fingers. But her silhouette quickly pulled out a long, thin weapon. She raised it over her head.

Just then, the silhouette of Professor Plum appeared behind the silhouette of Mrs. Peacock. In the nick of time, he grabbed the weapon away from her.

In the course of the struggle, each of the six weapons had been used only once.

WHICH WEAPON DID PLUM TAKE FROM MRS. PEACOCK?

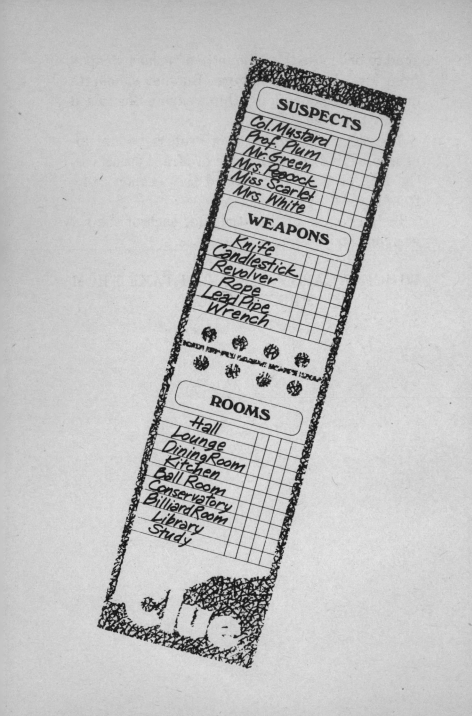

SOLUTION

The LEAD PIPE

The only weapon Mrs. Peacock could have used to burn a hole in the film is the Candlestick. We also know that she used the Wrench, the Rope, and the Knife. The only other weapon that could be described as long and thin is the Lead Pipe.

6.
Plum's Plasma

"**E**UREKA!" CRIED PROFESSOR PLUM, from one of the mansion's nine downstairs rooms. "I finally remember what I was doing! A science experiment!"

Plum had been standing in the middle of the room lost in thought over this puzzle for several hours. Now he rushed to the fireplace, where a pile of logs was burning. He carefully placed a glass beaker on top of the flaming logs. A mysterious purple solution was inside the beaker.

Plum waited for the solution to boil. It didn't. "A watched beaker never boils," he reminded himself. He closed his eyes. Instantly, the liquid bubbled and hissed and boiled violently. "Amazing," said Plum. "Those old sayings really work!"

He removed the beaker and set it down on the floor.

Using an eyedropper, Plum carefully removed some of the hot purple fluid. He gently squeezed the eyedropper's rubber bulb until a single, gleaming purple droplet emerged from the eyedropper's glass tip. He squeezed a little harder, and the purple droplet fell onto an empty glass petri dish.

Instantly, the liquid hissed and sizzled and, in a flash, turned into . . .

Purple plasma.

"Plum," Plum told himself, "you're a genius."

The professor walked to the mirror and stared admiringly at his own image. Then he frowned. Something was wrong. He saw what it was. He unpinned his purple bow tie from the top of his head and tied it back around his neck. "A genius," he repeated proudly.

He marched straight to the Billiard Room. Inside, the other guests were gathered around the billiard table, watching a game between Miss Scarlet and Colonel Mustard.

"Ahem," said Plum, clearing his throat.

He said it quietly, but the sound was just loud enough to throw off Colonel Mustard's concentration as he lined up his shot. His cue stick dug a deep scratch in the table's green felt.

"Sorry," said Plum. "It's just that . . . I've just discovered —"

"Not now," barked Mustard.

"But I've made the most amazing discovery. I've found —"

"Quiet!" Mustard ordered.

"Right," said Plum, who began talking very quietly.

Miss Scarlet lined up her next shot. She

bounced the white ball off the blue ball off the green ball off the purple ball off the red ball. Every ball rolled into a pocket except the black eight ball.

"I've been snookered," cried Mustard as the other guests applauded.

"Thank you, thank you," said Professor Plum, who had been talking very quietly this whole time and assumed the guests were clapping for him.

"Thank you for what?" asked Mr. Green.

"For what I just told you. I have just found an instant cure for . . ."

"For?" asked the guests.

Professor Plum scratched his head. "Ah, yes! For cuts and wounds," he finished with great pride.

"Watch this," he said. He reached into his pocket and pulled out the Knife with a great flourish. It was such a great flourish, in fact, that he lost his grip on the Knife, and it went flying across the room with tremendous force. Right at Mrs. Peacock.

She ducked, and the Knife sliced off the peacock feather that stuck up from her hat.

It kept going, and shaved off half of Mustard's mustache.

Then it whistled right around Mr. Green's head. Mr. Green tried to turn his head around quickly to watch the weapon, but he pulled a muscle and his head froze at an odd angle.

The Knife continued. It cut Mrs. White's shoelaces in half, whittled the top of Miss Scarlet's cue stick, and snipped off one of the buttons on Mr. Boddy's shirt. Then it hit the eight ball on the billiard table, knocked it into the side pocket, and caromed upward.

"What a shot!" Plum said with amazement. "Where did it end up?"

As if in answer, Colonel Mustard began to stagger around the room. He was holding his leg. The guests screamed.

"Don't worry," Mustard told them. "No cause for alarm, I just seem to be . . . dying."

"Oh, my goodness!" said the horrified Professor Plum. "I am *so* sorry. But there really is no need for alarm, Colonel. It just means I will get a chance to demonstrate my new cure. One drop of my magical mysterious purple plasma and you will be cured instantly. Faster than that, even."

"Well, don't just stand there," ordered Mr. Green, his head still stuck at a crazy angle. "Go get the cure!"

"Yes, my good man. Perhaps you should," agreed Mustard, who continued to stagger around the room. He was holding one hand over his missing half a mustache and the other over his leg wound.

"The cure!" agreed Mrs. Peacock, who looked rather odd with a one-inch feather sticking out of her cap.

"The cure!" echoed Miss Scarlet, pointing her broken cue stick.

"The cure!" said Mrs. White, whose shoes were falling off.

"The cure!" added Boddy, whose unbuttoned shirt revealed a big white undershirt.

"The cure!" yelled Plum. He turned to run. But he didn't run. He just stood there with a strange expression on his face.

"The cure!" said all the guests at once.

"The cure!" answered Professor Plum.

Everyone waited.

"Professor," Mr. Green said icily, "you do know where you left the cure, don't you?"

"Of course I know. I just can't remember."

Then, he ran out of the room, and the guests ran after him. They began searching room after room.

"No hurry," called Mustard, as he staggered after them. "I'm sure I can last a few more seconds."

He fell to the floor, then staggered to his feet again. Then he fell to the floor again.

Professor Plum had run right into him.

"Sorry!" Plum said.

Colonel Mustard lay on the floor. He beckoned Plum closer with a finger. "Think," he whispered in Plum's ear.

"About what?"

"Think about what room you were in when you had the cure."

Plum described his experiment. He described looking in the mirror.

"Great," gasped Mustard. "That could be the Hall, the Study, the Conservatory, the Dining Room, or the Kitchen."

"I remember there were pictures on the walls," Plum said.

"Great," whispered Mustard. He was fading fast. "That could be the Lounge, the Dining Room, the Study, the Billiard Room, the Conservatory, the Library, or the Ball Room."

"I remember the room had a door," remembered Plum.

"Great," said Mustard. "That could be the —" He stopped. "*Every* room in the mansion has a door, you numbskull."

He said it very quietly.

"I remember the room had a vase of flowers in it."

"That could be either the Kitchen, the Dining Room, the Lounge, the Hall, the Study, or the Library," said Mustard in the faintest of voices.

"I used the fireplace," added Plum.

This time Mustard only mouthed the words. No sound at all came out. If it had, he would have said, "That could be either the Study or the Library."

Then his eyes opened wide. He sat up straight. "I've got it!" he cried with a last burst of strength. "I know where you left the cure. It's . . . in . . ." He fell back.

"Where?" Plum yelled, shaking the Colonel.

"In . . . the . . ." Mustard's voice grew fainter and fainter. He began to mouth the last word.

But his mouth froze before he could finish.

IN WHAT ROOM DID PLUM LEAVE THE PURPLE PLASMA?

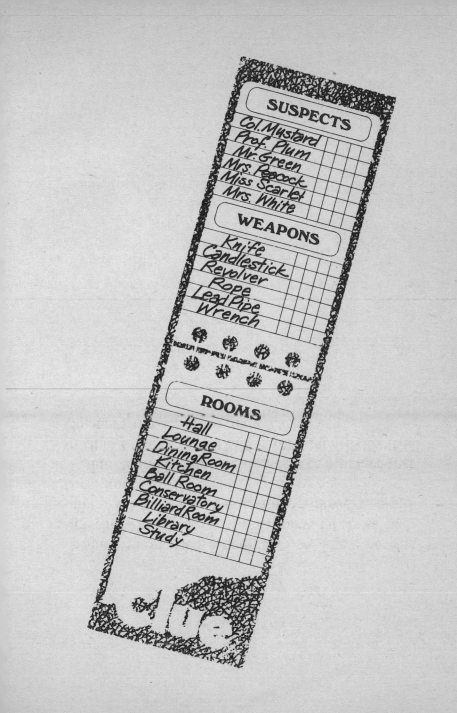

SOLUTION

The STUDY

Since Plum used a fireplace, we know he was in either the Study or the Library. Of these two, only the Study also has a mirror, flowers, a picture, and a door. Plum found the cure and gave it to Mustard just in time to save him. (But it took months for the Colonel's mustache to grow back.)

7.
A Show of Talent

"**P**RESTO-CHANGE-O!" SAID MR. BODDY. "Hocus-pocus, the hand is quicker than the eye!"

He was in the Kitchen, doing a magic trick for Mrs. White. He flipped the quarter from his left hand to his right. Then he opened his right hand. Empty. Then he opened his left. Empty as well.

"Amazing!" exclaimed Mrs. White. Then she turned away and rolled her eyes in disgust.

"Not bad, eh?" said Mr. Boddy with a proud chuckle. "Do you know where the coin went?"

"Behind my ear?" Mrs. White asked.

Mr. Boddy frowned. "Have you seen this trick before?"

"Never," promised Mrs. White. Then she turned her face to the side and mouthed silently, "Only about a thousand times."

"Well, anyway," said Boddy, "that's only part of my act for tonight's talent show. I'm so excited, aren't you?"

Mrs. White nodded her head up and down and then, when Mr. Boddy looked away, she shook it from side to side.

The reason Mr. Boddy had looked away was that there was a loud crash in the Ball Room.

"That's Miss Scarlet, practicing her baton twirling," explained Mrs. White.

"Ah."

Then there were three loud crashes from overhead.

"Professor Plum practicing his juggling," said Mrs. White.

"Ah."

Then came a bang and a scream from the Conservatory.

"Colonel Mustard practicing his marksmanship," explained Mrs. White.

"Mm, yes." Mr. Boddy frowned. Then he looked at what Mrs. White was holding. It was the Lead Pipe.

"Um, is this part of your act?" he asked.

Mrs. White nodded. "I play it like a flute."

Mr. Boddy took the pipe and examined it closely. "Fabulous!" He smiled again. "Everyone is so talented," he said happily. "What a show it's going to be!"

Later that night . . .

Later that night, the guests all gathered in the Lounge for the show that was about to begin.

"Welcome to the first annual Boddy talent show," Mr. Boddy said, clapping his hands together in excitement. "I'd just like to remind all of you that I have a special prize for everyone who enters. So there will be no losers, only winners. And everyone will get along famously, agreed?"

"I'm going to win," Miss Scarlet predicted quietly.

"No way," bullied Green.

Soon the guests were all screaming about who was going to win. Mr. Boddy yelled for quiet, but nobody listened. Until —

BANG!

Colonel Mustard fired his Revolver into the air.

Everyone fell silent. "You may continue, sir," Mustard told his host.

"Thank you," said Mr. Boddy.

The bullet, meanwhile, had made a hole right above Boddy's head. It travelled through Boddy's upstairs bedroom, through his bed, through his teddy bear, through the attic, and finally, through the roof and into the open air.

It was raining, and a single stream of drops fell through the holes and plopped, one at a time, on Mr. Boddy's head.

Mr. Boddy continued with his speech. "As —" PLOP! "I —" PLOP! "was —" PLOP! "saying —" PLOP!

"Oh, dear," the host said. He moved away from the drip and pulled out a small piece of paper. He peered at it closely. "The first act will be performed by —"

PLOP! PLOP! PLOP!

The rainwater hit the paper. All the guests' names ran together. "Yes, well." Mr. Boddy crumpled the note. "The order isn't important, I guess."

"You go first, Reg," cooed Miss Scarlet, draping one end of her red boa around Boddy's neck and pulling it gently back toward her. Except that it caught on his collar and nearly pulled him to the ground.

"Yes, Mr. Boddy, the show was your idea. It's only right that you begin," agreed Mrs. Peacock.

"All right then," Mr. Boddy said proudly. "Now, I know I'm not as talented as all of you. But I have been practicing a few magic tricks."

"Oooohh," said the guests.

"For my first trick, I will make a coin disappear." He reached into his vest pocket. Then into his left pants pocket. Then his right. "That's funny," he muttered with a scowl.

The guests applauded wildly. "Look at that!" said Mrs. Peacock with admiration. "He *did* make it disappear."

"Yes . . . er . . . isn't that strange? . . . I was

sure I had it right here. . . . Um, Colonel Mustard? Perhaps you would like to go first while I continue my search."

"Of course." The Colonel marched around the room, handing out small white cards to each of the guests. Each card had a tiny black diamond on it. "All right, I want everyone to get in a straight line."

The guests all formed a straight line except for Plum, who made it crooked. Mustard straightened him out.

"Now hold up your cards," Mustard went on. "And be sure to hold them away from your body."

Mustard made his way to the front of the room and removed a small mirror from the wall. He turned his back to his audience, peered into the mirror, and aimed the Revolver over his shoulder. "All righty, hold your cards up high," he instructed.

Everyone held their cards as far away from their bodies as their arms would reach.

Mustard aimed ever so carefully. Then he fired. The bullet zinged backward at lightning speed, piercing the black diamond on each card. The guests applauded the Colonel. Only Plum did not clap.

Just before Mustard shot, Plum, who was on the end, forgot why he was holding his arm in the air. He stepped forward to see what he was holding in his hand.

The bullet pierced the black diamond.

And then it pierced Plum's purple sweater, just over his heart.

ZING!

The bullet struck the Wrench in Plum's breast pocket and stuck safely between the Wrench's jaw. The startled Professor sat down in a daze, holding his purple hanky in one hand and mopping his brow with the other.

"Are you all right?" asked Mr. Boddy.

"Oh, yes, yes," Plum said bravely. "Don't worry about me. The show must go on and all that."

"I'll go next," said Miss Scarlet, who was wearing a cheerleading outfit made entirely of dazzling red sequins. She began twirling the golden Candlestick with amazing speed.

"Fabulous!" cried the delighted Mr. Boddy.

At least he was delighted until Miss Scarlet accidentally twirled the Candlestick right into his head.

When he regained consciousness, he said, "And now may I present Mr. Bean, I mean Mr. Mean, I mean . . ."

"Mr. Green," said Mr. Green. He pulled out a long yellow Rope and a small plastic statue of a cow. "Here's a rope trick," he said gruffly. He handed the statue to one of the women. "Hold that, please," he asked. "Watch me rope the cow." Then he made a lasso, whirled it around his head three times, cried "Yeehah!" and flung the Rope at the small statue of the cow.

He missed, but roped the woman and tied her up tightly before he realized his mistake.

When she was finally untied, Professor Plum performed his juggling act. He juggled the Knife, the Candlestick, and the Wrench. His act went brilliantly — until his mind wandered a little bit and the weapons all went flying into the air. They came down and clunked two of the men, right smack on their noggins.

Mrs. White went next. "I'm going to play this Lead Pipe like a flute," she announced. She put her lips to one end of the pipe and blew. No sound came out. She looked surprised and blew harder. Still nothing. Harder. Now her cheeks were turning red. She blew with all her might.

Until finally . . .

Mr. Boddy's disappearing quarter suddenly reappeared. The quarter had been stuck inside the Pipe, and now came flying out and thwacked one of the guests in the forehead.

Mrs. White couldn't see who she had just hit because the other guests had all gathered around their fallen friend. But she knew who it was.

Everyone but Mrs. White had now been wounded once, including Mr. Boddy.

WHOM DID MRS. WHITE HIT? COLONEL MUSTARD, MR. GREEN, OR MRS. PEACOCK?

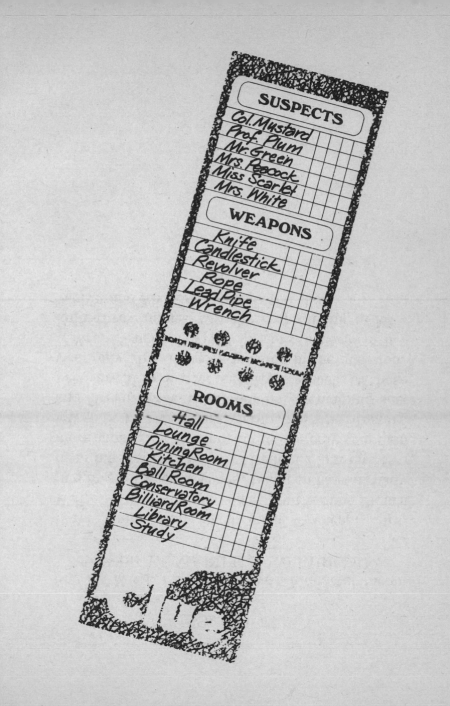

SOLUTION

She hit MRS. PEACOCK with a quarter blown from the LEAD PIPE in the LIBRARY.

We know that each guest — except Mrs. White — was wounded once. By the time Plum's juggling act goes haywire, two men have already been hit — Plum and Mr. Boddy. Plum hits two more men. At the time, there are only two men left to be hit, so Plum's victims must be Mustard and Green. That means our only remaining suspects are Miss Scarlet and Mrs. Peacock. Of these two, only Mrs. Peacock is listed in the question. Mrs. Peacock revives in time to perform her knife-throwing act. But she keeps aiming at Mrs. White, and Mr. Boddy stops the show.

8.
Trick or Treat

IT WAS A DARK MOONLESS NIGHT.

At the vast twelve-gabled Boddy mansion, the lights were all off. That's because it was Halloween. Mr. Boddy was expecting guests, and he had decorated the mansion for the occasion. In each of the large, spooky rooms, a jack-o'-lantern cast its flickering glow. Cobwebs hung from the ceiling. Everywhere you turned there were black widow spiders and furry vampire bats and large sharp-toothed rats — all stuffed, of course.

Someone was banging hard on the mansion's door knocker. The hollow knocking sound echoed through the huge, dark house.

Then came the sound of footsteps. A pirate with a black eye patch and one wooden leg hobbled in from the Kitchen.

Then came more footsteps. A glow-in-the-dark skeleton entered from the Study.

"Our first guest," said the skeleton eagerly. "Isn't this exciting, Mrs. White?"

"Yes, Mr. Boddy," said the pirate. "But remember," she added in a low voice. "My name's

71

not Mrs. White. It's One-Eyed Jack, the meanest scalawag who ever sailed the seven seas."

The skeleton roared with delight. "Yes, yes, quite right, I forgot. And you can call me —" He gestured at his glow-in-the-dark costume. *"Noboddy!"*

The knocking continued. "Will you two stop congratulating each other and open the door already!" yelled the angry voice from outside. "It's cold out here."

"Oh dear, yes, we forgot," said the skeleton. He opened the door.

The pirate screamed. The skeleton gasped.

There stood a vampire with a black cape and fangs that dripped with blood.

The skeleton laughed happily. "Come in, come in! Make yourself at home. Mrs. Whi —, I mean, One-Eyed Jack will fix you some punch."

"I vant blood," the vampire said, "not punch."

"Right this way," said the pirate, leading the vampire off to the Dining Room.

The skeleton was about to follow when the door knocker sounded again. He opened the door and in walked a witch with a broomstick.

"I hope I'm not late, Reg," said the witch, pinching the skeleton's cheek with two icy fingers. "I flew here as fast as I could."

"Flew here . . . ha-ha! . . . yes," said the skeleton happily. "You can, um, hang your broom in the Hall closet. Witches' brew is being served in the Dining Room."

The witch nodded and headed off into the shadows. Just then, someone knocked at the door again. This time it was a mummy.

"Mummy!" said the skeleton, opening his arms wide.

"I'm not your mummy," the mummy hissed.

"Well, just who *is* under all those bandages?" asked the skeleton happily, trying to peer into the mummy's dark eyeholes.

"That's a mystery you'll have to *unravel* yourself," the mummy answered.

The door knocker banged again, and the skeleton opened the door.

There stood a huge man with two heads. Each head had a Knife sticking through it. Blood, brains, and gore streamed down from both faces. "Pardon me," said the two heads at once. "But is there a doctor in the house?"

The skeleton couldn't stop laughing. "Such wonderful costumes," he said. "Just look at this mummy outfit." He turned to introduce the mummy. But the mummy was gone.

"This is no costume, you pea brain," yelled both heads. "We need a doctor!"

"Sorry!" cried Boddy. "My mistake. I'll call for one at once."

"Gotcha!" said the two heads, laughing.

The skeleton looked confused, then laughed, too. "We're all gathering in the Dining Room," he said, "and then we're going to do some trick-or-treating and then there's bobbing for apples and —"

The skeleton looked around in surprise. The two-headed man had tiptoed off while he was talking.

And when the skeleton searched for his missing guests, he found no one.

"Oh, I get it," the skeleton said. "A little game of hide-and-seek. How marvelously eerie!"

He tiptoed off toward the Lounge. "Come out, come out wherever you are!" he called.

The witch, meanwhile, was tiptoeing toward the Conservatory. She flung open the door and yelled, "BOO!"

But there was no one in the Conservatory. The witch entered stealthily, closed the door behind her, and waited for other guests to come in so she could scare them.

While she waited, her face began to itch. She pulled up her green rubber witch face and scratched with a long red nail. Just then, a gust of wind caught the candle in the jack-o'-lantern. The flame danced wildly and, for an instant, the light fell across Miss Scarlet's face. She quickly pulled her rubber witch face back into position. She watched the door closely.

So closely, in fact, that she didn't see the secret panel slide open. Nor did she see it slide shut again. Ever so quietly, the mummy had entered the room through the secret passageway from the Lounge. The mummy tiptoed up behind the witch and screamed, "BOO!"

The witch fainted.

"Ha-ha-ha!" the mummy chortled. "Got her but good." Then he crept into the Hall. He flung open the door and yelled, "BOO!"

But there was no one inside. The mummy went in and waited behind the door.

Suddenly, he heard a strange sound. A sort of *whoo!* sound. Someone had blown out the candle in the jack-o'-lantern.

The mummy grabbed for the door, and heard a click. The door was locked!

The mummy turned and groped his way toward the light switch, and got tangled up in spiderwebs.

He almost screamed. But then he remembered it was Halloween. They weren't real spiderwebs, they were just decoration.

Just then, a spider crawled across his cheek. He screamed and rushed for the light switch.

When the lights came on, he was staring straight into —

The razor-sharp fangs of the vampire.

The mummy screamed again and, as the vampire bit into his neck, he fainted.

"Poor professor," said the vampire in a man's voice. "Just vait till I tell the Colonel about this!"

Meanwhile, the skeleton was sitting in the Kitchen drinking a cup of punch. "I'll tell you, trying to figure out which guest is which is almost impossible," he told the pirate. "You'd think with only five guests, it wouldn't be so hard to figure out."

"Now let's see," the pirate said. "There's the vampire, the mummy, the witch, and the man with two heads. There must be one more."

"No, that's it," said the skeleton.

"But that's only four. We're either missing a guest or there are two guests in one costume."

"No wonder both heads were able to talk," the skeleton said.

"I know which guest is wearing which costume," announced the pirate proudly.

WHICH GUEST IS WEARING WHICH COSTUME?

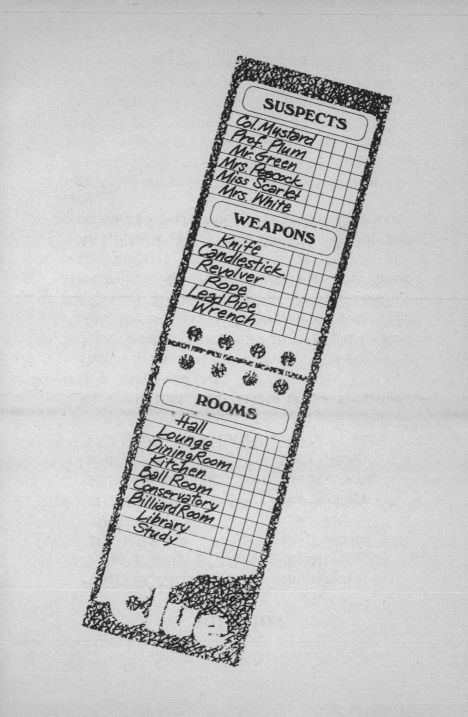

SOLUTION

MISS SCARLET   the Witch
PROFESSOR PLUM
MR. GREEN   the Mummy
MRS. WHITE   the Vampire
MR. BODDY   the Pirate
MRS. PEACOCK   the Skeleton
and   the Man with
COLONEL MUSTARD   Two Heads

We know that Mrs. White is the pirate and Boddy is the skeleton.

Thanks to an itchy mask, we saw that the witch is Miss Scarlet. Then the vampire told us that Plum is the mummy. He says he can't wait to tell the Colonel. Since Boddy is the skeleton, the only other male is Mr. Green. That means that Green is the vampire.

And Mrs. Peacock and the Colonel, our two remaining suspects, must have been sharing a costume.

9.
The Wrong Briefcase

"**A**S YOU KNOW, MY LECTURE TONIGHT is called . . ." Professor Plum paused and smiled blankly at the other guests.

"Relativity," whispered Mrs. White.

"Ah, yes, thank you. My lecture tonight is called 'Relativity: Why Aunts and Uncles Love to Pat Children on the Head.' "

The guests were all assembled in the Study.

"Lights, please," the Professor called.

Mr. Boddy turned the lights off.

"First slide, please," called the Professor.

Mrs. White flicked on the projector. The first slide appeared on the screen.

"And this . . ." Professor Plum stared at the white-haired man on the screen. "This is my uncle Harvey."

"It's Albert Einstein," corrected Mrs. Peacock.

"Quite right," said Professor Plum, studying the screen more closely. "I was, er, just testing you."

"Why don't you use your lecture notes, good man," suggested Colonel Mustard.

"Yes, yes, perhaps I had better. Lights, please."

Mr. Boddy turned the lights back on, and Professor Plum picked up his black briefcase. He popped the snaps, and flipped up the leather lid. Then he gasped.

There were notes inside, but not the right kind. Inside was a million dollars in cash!

"Oh, no!" cried Plum. "I took the wrong briefcase!"

The other guests gathered round in a circle, eyeing the money.

"Listen, old boy," said Mustard, "I don't know how good this lecture was going to be. But I must say, a million dollars makes up for the loss, doesn't it?"

"Not at all," said Plum huffily. "Darn!" He tearfully explained what must have happened. "You see, I went to the bank today. When I left, I realized that I had forgotten my briefcase. I went back and was lucky enough to find it still sitting there. But it wasn't exactly where I had left it. It was sitting right next to this very wealthy-looking gentleman who was on line to make a deposit."

"He's not wealthy anymore," said Mrs. White.

"I'd better call the bank," said Plum, snapping the briefcase shut again.

"Why?" said all the guests at once, so loudly

that Plum's glasses fell off his nose.

"To find out whose briefcase I have," he said, "so I can return it."

The guests led the professor to a chair and gently pushed him into it. "You dear, dear thing," said Miss Scarlet, trying to run her fingers through the few hairs on Plum's head. "You've had such a hard day, you're not thinking clearly."

"Yes, Professor. Giving away money is bad business," advised Mr. Green.

"Calling at such a late hour would be rude," added Mrs. Peacock.

"You deserve the money, to make up for losing your lecture notes," chimed in Mustard.

"But I don't need so *much* money," said Plum.

"But maybe some of your friends could find a use for it," said Mrs. White.

"Your closest and dearest friends," said Miss Scarlet, moving closer and looking dearer.

"I'd better count it for you, sir," suggested Mrs. White, trying to gently remove the briefcase.

"Let's have Mr. Boddy put it in his safe, old boy," said Colonel Mustard, trying to pry the briefcase out of Plum's hands.

"You need someone with business sense who can manage the sum properly," said Mr. Green, biting Plum's fingers.

Suddenly Plum leapt to his feet. "You're right," he said.

"We are?" they asked.

"Yes. Absolutely. The right thing to do is to call the bank."

"Call the bank? But that isn't how we advised you at all," said Miss Scarlet.

"It isn't?" asked the forgetful professor.

"Good, good, yes, call the bank," said Mr. Boddy, who had been watching the whole scene with a worried frown.

Suddenly, Mr. Green snatched the briefcase from Plum and bolted for the door. He would have made it, too, except that Mrs. White rolled the tea cart toward the doorway, blocking his way.

Mr. Green landed smack on top of a tray of pastries and rolled straight into the Library. He smashed into the bookcase with a crash. All twenty-six volumes of Boddy's Encyclopedia Britannica landed on Mr. Green's head, one after another, A through Z. He was knocked unconscious . . . but he learned a lot from the experience.

The other guests had chased after him. Miss Scarlet grabbed the briefcase from the unconscious Mr. Green.

"Grabbing is rude," said Mrs. Peacock. "Now give me that briefcase and next time, say please."

Instead, Miss Scarlet turned to run. But Colonel Mustard grabbed the case out of her hands.

Now *he* turned to run, but Mrs. White grabbed the case out of *his* hands. She turned to run and . . . she did.

But Mr. Green was waking up at just that moment. He tripped her as she ran by.

The case flew out of her hands and was caught by Mrs. Peacock. Colonel Mustard and Mr. Green started toward her. "Help me, ladies," she called, tossing the case to Miss Scarlet.

"Go out for a pass," Miss Scarlet ordered Mrs. White. Miss Scarlet threw the briefcase, but Professor Plum came from out of nowhere and intercepted it.

"Now," he said, "I can do what I said I was going to do from the beginning. I'm going to call the bank."

"Good," said Mr. Boddy.

"WAIT!" the guests all cried at once. "You haven't finished your lecture."

Plum's cyebrows went up. First one. Then the other. Then the first one again.

"Yes," trilled Miss Scarlet. "We are all just so fascinated by what you were saying. Couldn't the cally-wally to the banky-wanky wait until after the talky-walky?"

"Sorry, but noey-woey," Plum said.

Colonel Mustard looked at his timepiece. "Drat. I've got to leave shortly, old chap. And I was so hoping to hear your talk."

"Well," Plum said, "I didn't know you were all so interested in relativity."

"Oh, we *are*," said the guests.

"Well, in that case, I guess I could call the bank right afterward."

The guests cheered and followed Plum back into the Study.

"Lights, please," said Plum.

Mr. Boddy turned off the lights.

"Second slide, please."

With the black briefcase resting safely at his side, Plum began his lecture. "This is my aunt Myrna, patting me on the head at a recent party."

"This relativity business is just fascinating," said Mr. Boddy, studying the screen.

He was the only one in the room who was paying any attention to Plum's talk. Everyone else was quietly arming himself or herself with one of the six weapons.

As Plum droned on, one of the women quietly pulled a gold-handled Knife out of its sheath.

Meanwhile, Mr. Green carefully loaded the Revolver. While a second woman uncoiled the Rope, another of the men slipped the Wrench under his shirt, and another woman gently tapped the Lead Pipe against her palm.

"Now this," said Professor Plum, "is my great-uncle Sylvester, who —"

Plum, himself, had taken one of the weapons for protection, but he never got the chance to use it. He didn't even finish his sentence. A guest walked up behind Plum and knocked him on the back of the head with the Candlestick.

WHO HIT PLUM?

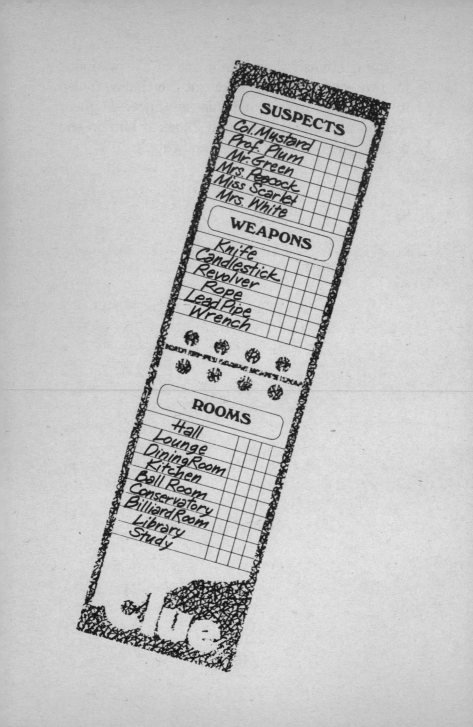

SOLUTION

COLONEL MUSTARD in the STUDY with the CANDLESTICK

All three women are accounted for — with the Knife, Rope, and Lead Pipe. We saw Green load the Revolver. We also know that it is a man who has the Wrench. Plum wouldn't hit himself in the head with the Candlestick. So he must have the Wrench. That leaves Colonel Mustard with the telltale weapon, the Candlestick.

When the lights came back on, the money was missing. Colonel Mustard got away with the theft, but the money turned out to be play money from a board game. Thanks to the missing notes and the knock on the head, Plum forgot his entire speech.

10.
Mr. Boddy's Pyramid

"**T**HIS WAY, THIS WAY," CRIED THE excited Mr. Boddy. "And no peeking!"

He was leading his visitors across the mansion's vast grounds. His five guests and Mrs. White, his maid, all followed behind, covering their eyes with their hands.

"And stop!" said Mr. Boddy.

But his voice was lost in a sudden gust of wind. And only plump Mrs. Peacock heard him. She was first on line right behind the host. She stopped. Colonel Mustard bumped into her. And Mrs. White bumped into him. And Professor Plum bumped into her. And Miss Scarlet — well, you get the idea.

The six people ended up forming a pyramid of tangled bodies. When they finally got to their feet again, Mr. Boddy said, "Well, what do you think?"

"I think I'm going to sue," said Mrs. Peacock, brushing off her modest blue dress.

"No, no, no," said Boddy. "What I meant was, 'What do you see?' "

The guests all peered around.

"Oooh!" cried Mrs. Peacock. "That *is* amazing."

"You think so?" said Boddy, beaming.

"Yes!" said Mrs. Peacock. Her head bobbed around like a bird. "Why, half the guests are wearing green shoes, and the other half are wearing white gloves. What a coincidence!"

"No, no!" said Mr. Boddy. "What do you see on the lawn that's new?"

The guests, who had been looking all around, finally looked straight ahead. Their mouths dropped open in perfect unison.

Behind Mr. Boddy stood a giant pyramid.

"What's an ancient pyramid doing here?" asked Mr. Green. "I thought these gizmos were found only in Egypt."

"It's not ancient," explained Boddy. "It's brand new. The workmen just finished laying the last block this morning."

"But darling, why would you want a pyramid?" asked Miss Scarlet.

"Well," said Boddy, "for the same reason the ancient pharaohs wanted theirs."

"Which was?" asked Mr. Green.

It was Professor Plum who explained, "The pharaohs built the pyramids as elaborate tombs."

"Just so," Mr. Boddy said. "You see, I wish to be buried here. . . . *After* my death, of course," he added with a chuckle.

Miss Scarlet threw her arms around her host's

neck and sobbed, "Oh, no, Reginald darling, you're not sick, are you?"

"No, no," Mr. Boddy said, smiling happily. "But," he added as soon as Miss Scarlet stopped hugging him, "we all have to go someday." Miss Scarlet wailed and threw her arms around his neck all over again.

"Now if you'll follow me, everyone," Mr. Boddy continued, "I'll give you a tour of the inside."

He led them to one side of the massive stone structure. There was no door in sight. "Here's the entrance," he said.

Mystified, the guests stared at the solid stone wall of the pyramid. "Where?" asked Miss Scarlet.

"Right here," said Boddy, tapping the stones.

Professor Plum, who had been daydreaming, walked straight into the pyramid wall. "Oof," he said as he bumped into it. When he turned around, his glasses were all crooked. "Trying to *brick* me, eh?" he said. "I mean *trick* me."

"Sorry," said Mr. Boddy. "I have to press the secret button. Everyone cover their eyes again."

The six bystanders all covered their eyes. (They also all peeked, as well.) Mr. Boddy pressed the corner of a high stone. A lower stone instantly popped out, revealing a control panel. He entered a code number, and six stones began to slowly slide away. Beyond lay a dimly lit passage.

Mr. Boddy led the way. The passage narrowed

as it approached a small golden door. Mr. Boddy turned to face his guests. "As you may or may not know," he said, "a pharaoh was buried with loads of gold and other treasure to keep him company in the afterlife."

"And, um, are you doing that part as well?" asked Plum.

"Yes. I figured, when you're buried in a pyramid, do as the pharaohs did. So I had the tomb filled with millions of dollars worth of treasure. I also installed a number of safeguards — dead ends, traps, that kind of thing — to protect me and my treasure after I, ah, can no longer do it myself. This way."

The guests were all wide-eyed. And there were little dollar signs in their pupils. Boddy entered another secret code and the short golden door swung open. Plump Mrs. Peacock went first, followed by Mrs. White and Miss Scarlet. "Watch your head," he warned both Colonel Mustard and Professor Plum, who ducked as they went through. Mr. Green and Mr. Boddy followed. Neither ducked. Mr. Green made it through fine, but Boddy smacked his head on the door frame.

After he stopped seeing stars, Mr. Boddy removed a golden Candlestick from a wall sconce and lit the candle. He led the guests through several twisting and turning passageways, up and down flights of stairs, and then through more passageways. Finally, they entered a small room. The guests gathered around him.

"Where is the treasure?" asked Miss Scarlet, looking around at the blank stone walls.

The room seemed empty, but it was hard to see by the low flickering light of Boddy's candle. The guests all peered into the darkness.

"There!" Plum pointed with a white-gloved hand.

But there was nothing but shadows.

"Actually, Mrs. Peacock is standing on it," said Mr. Boddy, grinning happily.

Mrs. Peacock stared down at her shiny green shoes and the stone floor beneath them. "I don't see a thing."

"Step back," Mr. Boddy warned. She stepped back. Then he pressed another button, hidden in a secret panel on the far wall. The place where Mrs. Peacock had been standing disappeared.

"A trapdoor!" all the guests exclaimed.

"And down through that trapdoor lies the treasure," said Boddy.

"Can we go down and see it?" Mrs. White asked.

"I'd rather not, if you don't mind," Mr. Boddy said. His voice broke. "I don't like to picture myself, well, you know, . . . dead. But you'll all see it when I *do* die. You're my closest friends, you see. The only ones I can trust with the secret of my tomb. So when I die, I want you to be the ones to bury me. I'll leave the map of the pyramid and all the secret codes in my will."

Miss Scarlet was sobbing again.

"Oh, now," Mr. Boddy said. "There's no need to cry, Miss Scarlet. I expect to live for a great many years."

But in truth, he had only one minute left. His last sixty seconds went by like this:

60 seconds: A white-gloved hand pinches out the candle in Boddy's hand. The tomb is now pitch black.

59 seconds: Guests gasp.

58 seconds: Mr. Boddy begins fumbling in his pocket for a match.

57 seconds: A green shoe kicks Boddy, sending him right into the open —

56 seconds: Trapdoor. Mr. Boddy falls through, as the Candlestick flies out of his hand.

55 seconds: Mr. Boddy lands with a thump.

54 seconds: The Candlestick lands on his head.

53 seconds: Mr. Boddy begins to crawl out of the innermost tomb and into a secret passageway.

44 seconds: He reaches the end of the passageway, just as —

43 seconds: Two slim women in green shoes roll

the large stone into place, blocking his way.

42 seconds: He starts crawling back the other way.

32 seconds: He gets back to the treasure room.

31 seconds: He remembers the matches in his pocket.

29 seconds: He strikes a match and sees —

28 seconds: A white-gloved hand about to stab him with a Knife.

27 seconds: He dives out of the way.

26 seconds: And lands on a second secret trapdoor.

25 seconds: And falls into another trap. A pit of venomous snakes.

24 seconds: He is bitten.

20 seconds: He manages to climb out of the secret escape hatch as the venom begins to take effect.

17 seconds: He swallows his special supply of snake venom antidote.

15 seconds: He rushes down a narrow secret passage, which leads him right back to the first golden door.

9 seconds: He pulls the door open, and sees —

8 seconds: A figure, standing up straight in the middle of the doorway. The figure's white-gloved hand holds a Revolver.

7 seconds: The figure fires once. Boddy screams.

4 seconds: The figure fires again. Boddy groans.

1 second: The figure fires one last time. Boddy opens his mouth but no sound comes out.

0 seconds: Mr. Boddy falls to the stone cold floor, stone cold dead.

WHO KILLED MR. BODDY?

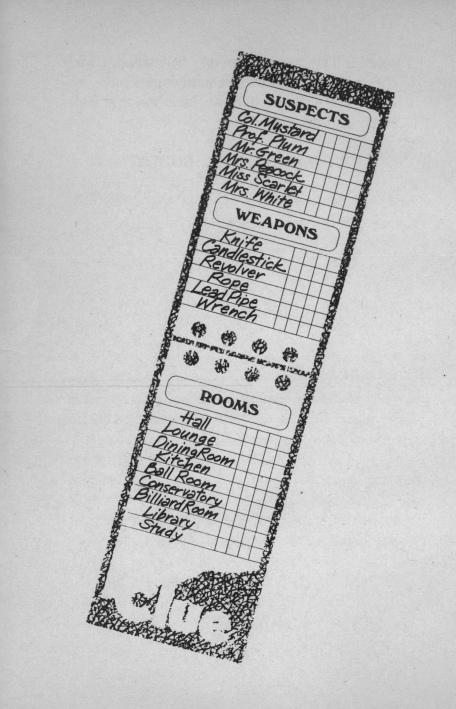

SOLUTION

MR. GREEN with the REVOLVER

We know that Mrs. Peacock wore green shoes. And we know she is plump. Two slim women in green shoes rolled the stone into place. Since only half the guests wore green shoes, this accounts for all the green-shoe wearers.

Of the men, Mr. Green is the only one short enough to stand up straight in the Golden Door-way. Green's height and white glove gives him away as the killer.

NOTES

NOTES

NOTES

NOTES